Little Ed and His Secret

Little Ed and His Secret

LORETTA CONNOR

authorHOUSE®

AuthorHouse™
1663 Liberty Drive
Bloomington, IN 47403
www.authorhouse.com
Phone: 1-800-839-8640

Published by AuthorHouse   07/27/2012

ISBN: 978-1-4772-5454-7 (sc)
ISBN: 978-1-4772-5453-0 (e)

Hi my name Ed I have a secret since I was little boy my secret was I had a disabilty and I over came it. It was so hard for me to go to school. I thought people would make fun of me when I frist started school. I had a friend that was right by my side through my young age her name is Lucy. my disabilty was speech and writing I was in a different class than everybody eise. My mom Kim is my best friend, and my dad Fred he is hard working guy. My disabilty was very hard on me. It took me.

A couple years to get through it. If anybody

has a disabilty you can do it just like I did.

Yes it will be hard but you will have family

and friend and your teachers to help. If it

was not my mom and dad my teachers I

would still have my disabilty I would not

have gotten it. My life is so much easier.

I am going in to the school and I still think

back about my disabilty.

Back when I had my disabilty kids would

pick on me because I was different and

they thought that I couldn't do what they

could do what they could. My speech and

my writing was not as good as theres. That is when I met Lucy and she helped me through it just like the teacher. I am a spanish boy I frist only 45 pounds when I frist started school. After I was born we moved alot only spending a year or two at one spot until we got here at mid-michigan but even then I haven't stayed in a single school for more than a year. We been in michigan for two years now I hope we stay so I went to ask my mom,dad if we can stay here until I get done with school they told me if everything goes right. school will be starting her in a couple days I have butterflys in my body we went to my school to met my teachers and the princical it is a big school I'll met new people and I don't know what they are going to stay to now here the people I met the frist day of scdool.

I remember the frist day I met Lucy. I was working on my writing she walked up and introdeuced herself. hi I'm lucy"

Hi my name is Ed, so how long have you been living in michigan.

He asked. I've been here for three years. Do you like living here so far?"

I don't know alot of people. but you will met alot people here and there," He assured he so do you have alots of friends

I wouldn't say alot friends but I have some." she responed

Do you thing they will like me "he asked

Yes" she stated bluntly

Evey throught I have problems?" he asked skepticley

Ed if any my friend pick on you I'll stand up to them," she said reassuring him, Ed do you want to go outside and play on the play ground?"

Yeah lets go play! Exclaimed Ed.

Hey, school will start here pretty soon do you want to meet my friend? "she excited Ed

Sure," he said nervously

Ok,let go!" said Lucy

Hey there's some kids, do you want to go talk to them?" he asked she smiled and asked

Hey you guys my name is Ed what is your name?he ask

What are you doing?" wondered Lucy

My name is Tony his name is Dan," Tony said we are just playing

Do you guys know Lucy?"

Yeah we've known her for two years. Dan said

I just moved here and am looking for new friends." Ed explained

Well we could be your friends too if you want." said Tony

Alright that would be cool. "Ed said "Well talk to you later then bye'

Yep. See ya." said Tony

Bye. "Lucy said waving

Lucy do you want to meet my baby sister?" asked Ed

Sure where do you live?" she responded

"In the little green house an hill like right over there." he said pointed toward his lelf

What your sister name?"

"shelly"

How old is Shelly?" Lucy asked

She's seven years old last june . . . I think."
he trying to remember

Hey! Lucy this is my mom "Kim and this
my dad Fred.

Mom where is Shelly? Ed asked she is in
her bedroom

"Hey" Shelly

"yes" Ed what do need. Lucy this is Shelly, Shelly this is Lucy. Hi Lucy Shelly said

Ed I have to go home now my mom wants me home at 4 pm. Ok Lucy "said" Ed

See you in school Ed" said Lucy bye said Ed

Bye Lucy "said Ed

Well it time for dinner Ed come set the table. his mom said

{next day of school}

I went to my class that Lucy was in. Ed said

Hi Lucy said Ed good morning said Lucy how are you doing?said Ed ok said Lucy

Hey Tony what are you doing after school today?ask Ed

 nothing why Ed. said Tony

I want to know if you hang out at my house for a couple hours Ed ask

Hey Ed I have to ask my mom and dad frist Tony said

That's cool "said Ed

{at lunch time}

Hey you guys,who that boy that sitting bye Lucy? ask Smith

That's the new kid the block his name is Ed. answered Big D

Should we go to talk to him and Lucy? ask Smith

No said Big D

Why not? said Smith

I heard that he can't talk english.Big D explaied

Smith and Big D who are you both talking about? ask Dan and Tony

Ed! Why do Ed why do ask

Is Ed spanish Tony? because he look like it he is.said Smith

Well it is the end of the day until tomorrow. said Ed

Hey Ed! "Smith yelled his name what Ed said" and who are you? Ed ask

My name is Smith. he said

So do you have any friends beside Lucy.

Smith asked

"Yes" I do Ed answered

When did you meet Lucy? Smith ask Ed

I met Lucy in the park couple of days befor

school started. Ed said

You know Ed! I don't think you should

have her for you friend. Smith explained

I have to go now Smith! so if you have to

stay anything else to me you can stay it

later.

bye Smith

Ed shows up at home

Mom I am home do you want me to do anything in the house befor I go outside to ride my bike. Ed said

"Yes" can you come here frist so I can talk to you?

Yes mom I can

The school called here today and they want you to talk about your disabilty with the princical. She want you to go see her when you get there.his mom said "ok" mom said Ed

Hey Tony do you know a kid name Smith?
he ask

"Yes" I do why?

He don't think Lucy should not be my
friend. Ed said

I have a scaret about me and the princical
know what it is. said Ed

Dose Lucy know what it is? Tony ask

"No" said Ed

Hey Lucy after school I have to talk to you about something. said Ed

Ok said Lucy

I have to go now said Ed

Bye Ed said Lucy

Ed we want you to talk to your class mates about you disabilty? ask the prncical

Why do I have to talk to my classmates for? If I stay anything I'll lose my friends. Ed explained

Ok Ed! If you not ready that fine with me. said the princical

Good said Ed

Lucy! If I tell you something you promise you won't laugh at me. ask Ed

I promise Ed I will not laugh at you your my best friend. Lucy said

Hey you two what are you doing?ask Dan

I am talking to Lucy about something. Ed said

Why? Do you want something. said Lucy

I want to know if you both want to come over later please? Dan ask

Let me ask my mom Ed said and Lucy said I have to ask too

Ok said Dan just let me in two hours please

"Yes" we can Lucy and Ed said

So Lucy this how it is I have a disabilty me speech and writing. said Ed

I know you have a speech problem since I met you by just the way you talked but that did not matter Ed. Lucy said

That good Lucy "Ed said

I have to go to the princical after school so I can tell her that I am ready to talk about my disabilty to the class

Thats a good idea Lucy replyed

But I don't want people think I am different because I am not Ed said

{Go to talk to the princical now}

Hello! Mrs Write

I am ready to talk now you make the day and I'll be there. he said

Ed you are doing the right thing Mrs Write said

"Yes" I know that. he said

Well you have to go now so you don't miss the bus Ed's princical replyed

Hay! mom I talk to Mrs Write I am going to talk to my class mates is that ok

Yes Ed she said

Can I go outside mom? he ask

Yes Ed you can she said

Thanks

after a few hours of playing

Ed it time to eat now. his mom said

Hay mom can you let know how I can put my disabilty into words when it's time to talked to my class mates "yes" I can she said

{The next day}

I went to the gym because this is the day I will talk about my disabilty. he said

Ed can I be right their when you do this ok. said ED

so it happen

There is alot of people here he said and my mom and dad is here to. Ed said

After I did it everyone came up to me and ask different thing

Ed! may I help you? he ask

Yes my name is Big D that what people calls me.

Why? he ask

Because my name is Derrick and i like big D

I had the sam promble when I frist started school to. Derrick said

Know one said anything to you about it. Ed ask

"Yes" he answered

How did you get through it? Ed said

I took it day by day Derrick said

What about Smith how long did it take you to get him for your friend? Ed ask

Not long I told him about my disabilty and he was fine with it. he answered

So you think Smith will be ok with me now or will it take more time?Ed asked

Ed let me talk to Smith and see what he think frist. ok

"Yes" he answered

Well I think my mom and dad want to go now I have to see my doctor

Ok Ed see you later. bye Ed said

Hay! Ms. Write

'Yes" Ed

Did I do good today?

Yes you did. she replyed

In the car on the way to see the doctor

Mom can we go out to eat tonight?

Let see what we have after yours and Shellys doctor opointment. his mom said

{The next day at school}

Hay!

Ed! yes Smith

That was a good Speech yesterday

Thanks you! Ed answered

Hay! you guys what are you two doing?Tony and Dan yelled out

Ed are you ok? yes I am. he said

So Smith did you change your ways about Ed yet? the boy said

"Yes" I have

I should got to know Ed befor I talked about him like that. Smith said

My disabilty is part of me and people have to talk to me frist befor they say anything. Ed replyed

You know Ed Tony and Dan I fell so bad what I did Big D talk to me yesterday after school. Smith explained

There is Big D now. Ed said

"Derrick"

Yes Ed what can I do for you? ha ask

I am so happy now because you all my friend I thought no one will like me. he said

Well Ed you have more friends now then

you walked that door. the guys said

I have to go fine Lucy I'll see you guys

later. he said with smile

bye Ed they all said

 bye Tony, Dan, Smith and Derrick

Lucy! he yelled out

Who yelling at me. she answered

"me"

Oh hi Ed!

Hello! Lucy I have something to tell you. he said

What's that Ed. Lucy smile

Smith and Big D is my friend now I talked to Smith just a few minuts ago Big D was yesterday

That is the best news I'll heard all day Ed. she responded

I fell like I want to jump up and down and yell but I know we can't yell in school.Ed said

Ed you can do that when we get out school today. she replyed

The end of the day

What are you doing after school today? ask Ed

I have to go home because I have to watch my sister and my brother for two hours.Lucy responded

How many sister and brother do you have?Ed ask

I have two sister and three brothers. Lucy said

Ok Lucy see you later. he said

{On my way home}

Shelly!

What do you want Ed. he ask

I have to help my mom with the house frist. Shelly responded

That right I have to clean my room. Ed said

"Ed"

Yes mom

Can you help Shelly with the dishes? his mom ask

Do I have to mom?

If you don't you will be in the house for today. she said

Ok mom I'll do it. Ed said

After I get done. Can I go outside please? Ed ask

"Yes"

{Three hours later}

It's time to come in the house now.

Can you and Shelly get the table ready to eat? ask his mom

"Yes" We can they said

{The next day of school}

Ms Write

Can I talk to you for a couple minutes I have to ask if I can do something? he ask

What that Ed she wonder

This is frist year can I start helping other with there disabilty. he smie

Ed you have a long way for you get better with your disabilty befor you help other people. she resopnded

Yes I know that Ms Write all I want to do is to talk to other kids that have disabilty. he said

Let me think about it.she said

That's fine let me know soon. he said

Well you have to go to class now. she said

"Tony"

Yes! Ed

What are we doing in class today. Ed wounder

Nothing we going watching a move. Tony responded

That sweet. he said

I am so mad. Why? Tony

Because I want to talk to Ms Write to see if I can talk to other kids about their disabilty.in sad voice

You have to let your disabilty get better befor you help anybody else. help yourself frist.Tony responded

Thank you Tony he said

Were is Lucy? do you know? Ed ask

Yes I do Ed why? Tony ask

Just what to know

Shes at home Lucy is sick don't know how bad she is. Tony said

That not good I might go over there and talk to her mom. said Ed

Ed don't go over. why? Can't you call her when you get home today.he said

Hay! Tony I think that is a good idea so I won't come come down sick either. he said

{ Going to lunch}

Hay! Ed

"Yes" Smith

How is your disabilty doing and who helping you with it? ask Smith

Everybody is helping out. Its going to take time my writting is getting better now. Ed responded

{Back to class}

I wish Lucy was here Ed said to himself

Why that Ed? ask Dan

Because she the only one I can talk to when I need to talk. Ed said

You know you can talk to me.

Yes I know I can but i knew Lucylonger thin anybody. he said

But can I ask what you want her for Ed?

So how bad do you want to know?and why? I know you are my friend too.he responded

Ed I want to be their for you. But I know Lucy has been there for you longer but I can listen too. I think of as my own brother. said Dan

Yes I know Dan. I don't have a brother I have a sister that why I know should open up to you. So I will try. Ed said

Ok we can talk about it later. I'll let you go so you can clear your head frist. Dan said

See you later Dan thanks for talking to me. he said bye

Bye he said

{time to go home}

Hello! mom how was your day today?

"Good" his mom said

Lucy wasn't at school today she is sick can I call her after dinner please? ask Ed

Yes you can but don't be on the phone to long. she said

Thanks mom your the best and I love you. he said

Shelly!

Yes! do you think you and Ed can set the table for dinner please?she ask

Yes but did you ask Ed yet? she ask

No! but I will ask him now. her mom said

Ed

Yes mom

Help Shelly set the table?she ask

"Ok"

It is time to eat go and get your dad.she said

So dad how was you day at work?Ed ask

It was ok. But I am tired.

{After dinner}

Can I call Lucy now mom? he ask

Yes Ed

{Two hours later}

Shelly do you want to play on the game with me?he ask

Yes just a short because I want ti go to bed early. she responded

Ed what game do want to play?

We can play on playstion 2. But we can play the snowboarding game ssx2. he said

Sound good to me. she said

Hay! you two I play the winner. there dad said

We can do that dad. they said

Good

Mom can we have a snack please? he ask

I don't care what do want? she said

"Popcorn"

Dan do want to take over because I am going to bed now.she said

Yes I will but we are not going to be on it that much long. he said

Dad how much longer?" he ask

One hour because you have school. his dad said

Dad can I talk to you after this game? "Ed ask

Yes my son

I have this boy at school that wants me to talk to him more but I don't know if I want to or if I should.What do you think?

Well son it all up to you is he one of your friends and how do you get along with is he like Lucy?he ask

He is one of my best friends. Ed said

Then you do what is best for you.Not for him. he said

I like Dan but what I have to say to Lucy it's between me and her not Dan. Ed answered

Time to go to bed we will talk more when you come home from school.

Yea! dad thats ok your the best.

You are so welcome.

{Next day}

I know I talk to my class mates already but now I want to talk to the whole school now? Ed ask

We have to askMs Write and see what she say about it. she responded

Ok! Can you let me know I want to be at the end of the school year.

Yes! I let you know Ed.

Now I have to find Lucy.

I think she is in the back room Ed.

Lucy how are you doing today?Ed ask

I want to know if you will help me with my math because I don't understand it.

Yes! I can help you. When dose it have to be tured in?

Later in mathclass. he smile

Ok"

{Lunch time}

Ed want are you doing? ask Tony. I'm doing my math it's do next class.

Have you see Lucy?

No" Why

She going to help me. he said.

I think she in the office.

Ok! can you help me please?

Yea!

"Thanks"

We have five minuts befor class starts. Ed said

I know you have a few more and that it. Tony responded

Well time to go bavk to class now.

Ed you have to go see Ms. Write right now.said Mrs. Hall

By the way were is your math paper at frist?she ask

I have it right here. he said

Here is your pass to go.

Ms Write I am here. What do you need?

Your mom is herentopick you up. she responded

Why is she here?

You should askher Why Ms Write said

Hi! mom what going on. What are you doing here? Ed ask

I'll tell you in the car. his mom said

{In the car}

The doctor called the house and I need you come with me. she said

Why? did the doctor call for? And who is it for?he ask

"You"

What about me? he ask

They found something on your brain. his mom said

Do you know what is it yet? he ask

"No"

But he wants to see you now to check you out more. she said

Why do they have to see me for I feel healhy. he said

Just make sure you don't have anything else wrong with you. she said

Ok" I guess just to make you happy mom. he responded

Were here now so be good Ed and don't say anything to Shelly yet.

I won't momI promise Shelly is baby sister and I don't want her upset. with a sad face

{Later that day}

Shelly1 Ed haves cancer on the brain.her mom said

Is Ed going to ok. Shelly asked

Yes he is. But they think they cought it early. she said

Well Ed you have a tumer and you have to go through a operation very soon to remove it. his dad said

If I do go through this. Will my disabilty go away or what? ask Ed

I don't know Ed. he said

Let go and get some pizza for dinner and talk about it more. they said

Shelly! Are you ok? Ed ask

Yes! I am fine it won't be that bad you know mom,dad and I will be their for you. Shelly said.

"Good"

Mom do want me do anything? befor the night is over.

"No"

Just go play outside.

Thanks mom

Dan! What did we do in class?

Not much Dan said

Were did you go Ed? You were and then you were gone? Dan ask

Dan I can't say right now. Ed responded

Are you ok?

Yes

That is good

{ Three hours later}

I have to go home now Bye Dan see you in school. Ed said

See ya Ed have a good night. Dan said

By the way Ed! I heard Ms. Write and Mrs. Hall talking after school about you today after you left.

What did they say about me? ask Ed

They said you are going to talk to the whole school at the end of the week. about something. They didn't say what about.Dan said

I know what going on. Because I ask if I can talk about it now because I have more to say. Ed said

Are you going to do what? You been wanted to do when you frist got here? Dan ask

Yes I am Dan! and I have alot to say now. Ed responded

Ok

{ Later in that day}

Can we talk about what going on in this family mom and dad? ask Ed

Yes what do want to talk about Ed?they ask

Well what going on with me/ And can they do anything for me? Ed wonder

Ed we don't know yet It going take time. and we have to take it day by day. but it looks good.

Well we don;t have time. Our family always have bad news it not right, he said sadly

I know Ed it will get better. We love you both we won't let anything happen/ they responded

Thats good. mom and dad I am so happy you are here for me and Shelly. Ed said

Shelly what do you thing about this? mom, dad ask

I don't know what to think I just turned seven year old. she said

You don't have any question for us?They

ask

If I have any question I'll let you know.

she answered

Ok" Shelly

Its late let all get a good night sleep and

we talk after school. they said

{next day}

Hello! everybody.

Ed we have to go down to the gym are

putting chair in their now. said Mrs Hall

Why! I am doing it now why can't I do it friday? ask Ed

Because everybody wants to know whats going on with you. she said

Ok! Who is all going to be there everybody in the school? he wonder

Everybody from school and your parents will be here

"Ok" When do we start this so I can it done? he ask

One hour from now

Lucy were are you going to sit at?Ed ask

I am going to try to be close to the front. Is that ok?

Yes! as longs as I can see you I'll be good to go. he said

{Its time to talk to middle school and fifth grade}

Hi! My name is Ed Mac some of you know me but some of you don't. And I have a secret.. I have disabilty my disabilty is speech and write I just found out I have a tumer in my head. It is so hard to live when you know that you have a disabilty.

You have people picking on you and

they think you are so different. and if you

think about it your not thay different from

everybody else. My disabilty gets to me

all the time. I don't tell everybody but if

you havedisabilty or a tumer you can get

through it just like I am yes I will be going

through anoperation yes I have it still

befor you know it I will be one hunderd

precent better or at least I hope so. So if

you have a disailty you can get through

it just like I am so just remember don't

pick on someone else because theres

something wrong with them. try to be

their and talk to that person frist before you talk crap that how I see it. I had some one about me until he found out I have a disabilty and now he and I got to know me now he is my friend. So think about it impolite to other people. Thank you for listen to me.

the end

I hope this is a eye opener and you enjoy ready it my story and if you meet anybody with a disabilty don't pick on them or don't look at help them out.

author Loretta A Connor